THE ALLURING BRUME

SYED SAKISH BUKHARI

ISBN 979-888521815-3

Remembering...

The lauded mentor and inspiration

The Guide and the all-time heartthrob.

My Sacred Father

"Abu Ji"

Syed Ghulam Hassan

May His pious soul rest in peace.

"Abu, I will indeed carry you with me till I will see you again and your guiding hand will remain with me forever". You are the lifeline, the paladin and indeed my superhero.

Contents

Preface

Right from the Prologue of this anthology "The Alluring Brume" I have tried to verbalize the excitement and the perception of instant juvenile at the onset of respective sweet sixteen. The level of hysteria and absurdity to let your dignity get worn-out just from the inception. A sudden feeling what they call as "love at first sight", ends up on being just an effectuation. Indeed, throughout the boyhood this is an abiding course that gradually submerges your adolescence to the harrowing conclusions.

This Anthology will offer you a ground to heft yourself as a boy and intern will aid the guardians to envisage about the growth of at hand decedents.

Throughout the print, for my buoying and encouragement my admired and favorite people have reserved my morale and confidence for a finest conclusion and outcome.

About The Author

Syed Sakish Bukhari, in full Syed Najamul Saqib Shah Bukhari, born on 05 Sept.1995 in an abundant literate and panoramic hamlet Sogam lolab kupwara, J&K INDIA. "The Alluring Brume" is the debut fiction anthology published besides this syed sakish bukhari is rendering his eminent services as a tutor in Dept. of school education J&K INDIA and has created a decisive image in imparting the morality and rectitude among the students.

The Author from his early age has remained active in co-curriculum's and has been awarded severally for his decisive way of debating and unique gestures at local and national levels.

Moreover, the author is currently scripting some other titles,

Viz, **The Eve** (A book on Women Empowerment) and **"Gudgeon"** (Victims of journalism).

ABOUT THE AUTHOR

Syed Sakish Bukhari

Prologue

In the meanwhile, she started a chat with her exclusive tone. A soothing voice that hypnotized him to an extent. He started staring to have some relief to his excruciating sight. He recalled his recurrent dreams at the onset of his sweet sixteen, the brownish hair and the cherry cheeks, the rosy lips and the tulip chin, the carved cauline throat and the cute celestial nose all summing up to a vision of loveliness and the sight of sore eyes. In a go he got to know that he had found a jewel in a maiden go. The awful feeling like being raised from a caterpillar to a butterfly, feeling of happiness around even without seeking approval of the others, was all providing a positive vibe and intense energy to create a life that feels good on the inside. The life looked stand still from being a hodophile, everything looked so charming and real indeed without proper knowledge of how, when, from where.

He started assuming reality is finally better than the dreams. The smiling gestures from that luminous bloom was feeding euphoria to listen the vibes inside. That brad seemed enough to drive a saint to madness or a king to knees, seemed a ray of sun shine, an intense bright fire on a cold winter's day, she looked to Roy as though she lived in Oz, in the land of color.

The brume she sprinkled around and carried everywhere she went, was smelling alike alluring Aroma, attar, bouquet and fragrance that made him cognoscenti and his connoisseur nature assisted him to distinguish this redolence scent from anything that he had gasped so far. The intense bloom of that divine seraph got him to trust the divine attributes and epiphany of the exclusive conception and creation of the creator. In a first go, all his peripheral sensorium's started being occupied alike being alive and dynamic, with lone distinct direction forward to fabric an imposing subsequent. For this confrontation it seemed the divinity is doing the honors to mediate amidst.

1. First Sight

Gasped in awe, all stand still,
Instantly cherubim slaty claded,
Flickering ma perception,
Conjuring the subsequent,
Sparsely trifling chantant,
Splendid virtuous amble,
Thou dainty grin, glanced gaze,
Truly unearthed cosmos amaze,
Tingled awe seraph effloresce demeanor,
Contiguous covet apprise corporeal for,
Providentially juxtaposition I came,
Wandered off farrago muddle all the lame,
Pronto I desire yet flipside to acquire,
Thou winsome gracious ubiety of the exclusive brad.

How it commenced

The state of trepidation on the onset of conversation desisted soon with her inclusive gestures. To his "HI" she replied soberly like an infant bairn with "hello". This single word just vibrated his instincts like he found the peace amidst.

Actually, Social media played a role amidst to introduce "Panda" and "Boo".

The ordinary texts in the beginning soon sequel to the frequent chats, both had started affecting each other without a formal meet.

2. Enduring the brouhaha

Instantly discerning floret, fixating vine,
Halted viable, cognizant existence mine.
Doubting animate with twitching compassion,
Staring alongside with fondness and passion.
A desire to verbalize myo sound off plus hi,
However, quivering for conceding of why.
Neither on the boat, never on the sail,
Being afraid of ache, and appalling fail.
Yet not cogitating for close by subsequent,
Sole deed of inclination with all my intellect.
Acquiring fortitude to reveal the notion,
Pausing the aggregate, producing the motion.
Shuttering the gaze, declaring the whole,
Murmured my hunch, and focal soul.

The Excitement amidst

Boo remembering an incident…

The Annual semester exam for Panda is commencing and she the luminous floret is busy as usual with her social media handles, boo on the other hand being extra protective, crossing her to put the phone down and to engage herself in preparations. Panda the seraph is coddled by everyone for being the dearest and divine with her conduct. Nobody, yes literally nobody has even shouted on panda so far and the boo crossing her in a first should have enraged her, but no it is the first time when she is getting influenced by other who is yet just an Instagram buddy to her. On the caution she just replied "ok I will" and like seriously she put her phone down and looked for the books and the other material, as boo got the confirmation regarding the same from her Cuzz later…

AWWWWWWWWWWWWW <3 So sweet na!

She confessed at various intervals that yes boo affects her and indeed it was true on the Vise Versa. Like usual it was not the Panda and Boo right from the beginning but instead on the onset it was just the title of the two Instagram profiles.

Wow he felt, in a while when the phone numbers got exchanged, and don't ask how relived he felt when his phone vibrated with panda on the screen. With tumbling hands, he popped the green icon up...

3. Ma Hon

Is it ok if I call you divine?
Is it ok if I sing you a rhyme?
Neither a flower nor a honey bee,
Prettier than both that only I can see.
Praising the Lord, for sending me you,
Applauding him for changing my view.
Love the way you grin at me,
Love the way you pamper me.
You are the one I can't live without,
This fact is true; I have no doubt.
Thoughts of you, surround me.
Love for you, defines me.
Pen and paper in front of me.
Trying to set all my feelings free.

The perception

Her hair swayed in the breeze, tickling the back of her neck.

She was walking through the out streaks of the countryside.

Boo, could only see her back from where he was standing, but by the curvature of her neck he guessed she was busy in updating her social media handles.

Yes, it had been 33 days, 17 hours and 13 minutes since this luminous bloom shared a snap.

And now he was frozen, unable to move

She looked so peaceful, so beautiful

So soft and distinctly different from the active tumbling state he was in.

And she hardly knows he was around.

-Boo-

I spent most of my evenings in the hammock, enjoying the late August sun

Today I was reading, but sometimes I'd knit, or draw, or just watch the birds

I was trying to take my mind off through continues thoughts of subsequent viz, when, how and where…!

But all of a sudden I heard a sound behind me, it was my phone vibrating for a visual chat…

“Panda!” I cried, all but falling out of the hammock

She gave me the biggest grin I’d ever seen, as she had seen her subsequent in me.

“I threw my arms around her, burying my face in her neck

And I started to sob with relief” keeping the camera off I was

Sobbing my mobile phone instead.

4. Sensing you

Talking with you is an honor.
Gazing on you is a wonder.
Imagining you just after feeling pure.
You are the perfect one, I am sure.
Holding you makes me feel safe.
Pampering you makes me feel great.
Can't think without you on mind.
Can't leave without feeling unkind.
I see you in my thoughts and dreams.
When I wake up all real it seems.
Everything else fades when you touch me.
I think I might fly when you grin me.
You are the one I was waiting all long far.
You have been a find I always cherish for.

The sprinkled brume

A good time has passed now, since two undiscovered Instagram buddies started texting each other, "boo" feeling the extreme now, tried several attempts to express his intentions but always worrying for the subsequent as he can't afford to lose a chum, who was the vision of sore eyes.

Something was not good as normal it all looked by the unusual texts amidst as for no society will ever bear or ratify such a kinda liaison, why so, it remained a secret throughout.

The inclination towards the bask was indeed accelerating with passing time and same was peeping from the other side too.

The boo crossing the barriers asked for something like if he is being cherished the same way, is it existing the same way there? how he has been prone here, are the perceptions same? blah blah...

For all these brainteasers, boo got a positive response. No doubt she replied in a tumbling state with, as she had not figured it so far but this time in a first he was titled as "You are my Secret personal diary I can't share even an inch of yours". The height of passion and predilection was that when "Panda" exclaimed that if ever "boo" departed or pulled out for any reasons whether on his or her side, she won't be living like a living being for the subsequent later!

Now, you decide was it enough for boo to lose his all heart and get in through?

Of course it was. The Boo being the Hodophile and nature lover got confined for what just Panda allows him to do.

Asking for to stand up?

Boo is standing!

Asking for to Sit?

Yes, sitting down highness.

Indeed, the blessings of divinity that boo thought he is baptizing with.

5. Demented Perception

While I think the love I am in,
Culture have declared it a sin.
You are in love with a psychotic clown,
Though what about that face that is not frown.
Not anyone discerns my plight, my pain,
Yet I was sure for nothing will go in vain.
Some titling crazy others call me Mad,
Seldom it matters for I love that exclusive brad.
Timid I am and tears I can never handle,
Anxious if you departed, with this I fumble.
Push me, hit me, but don't ever leave,
Even a little I won't hurt, in me believe.
You feed me wisdom, you make my day,
You decorate my dark world and every single day.

The Plight

All was calm and normal going,

You know what?

They literally had started dating each other Aaha!

Now the frequent meets, full night conversations Aaha!

Oh God please don't let any bad eye arouse.

"A day when both travelled for a long with hands shaking. It was indeed first time for both to stand so close physically. AWWWWW the aroma amidst, the feeling of oneness and the slow wind coming through the pane of the car was all providing a sense of being somewhere so far, so distinct, nobody is where, to disturb.

You know how it felt……!

Again that slow swaying of her hair was disturbing the floret and AWWWWW boo made her feel relaxed by sobbing her forehead and slowly wiping her brownish hair to her ears, she got blushed, it was worthy to be seen from her red rosy checks.

Time kept on passing with numerous promises viz, promises of being together forever, whatever the circumstances ought to be, the promises of believing in oneness and to stay focused towards the happening inclination and blah blah…

The stiff change in the attitude and to deal the things in boo was noticeable, as unusual of him he started to remain busy like in his own world without caring for a little. He was indeed witnessing a world around, by the presence of beloved.

Why and what he should care for...!

The issues common throughout the adolescence viz, Self-esteem and body image, stress, bullying, cyber addiction and most commonly the introduction to the harrowing drug consumption were all Boo had never thought about, even losing the parents at a quite early age.

The presence of panda was indeed never less than a fresh breath, at hand life and an exhalation, that boo always cherished for.

But his unfortunates………..

Oh Gosh...!

The worrying part that remained a secret throughout, now in a first started annihilating the effectuation amidst.

However even being discussed rigorously, Boo usually managed to get over the chaos and making everything look exquisite, but the spark was slowly igniting and God forbid if someday it flared up, indeed it gonna burn both the true soul, this agony was always a bruised thought.

The thought of being a cursed one was a recurrent speculation for boo, coz of various past harrowing episodes, and hence he was indeed timid this time too for his regular unfortunates and yes of course he had already made Panda aware about these occurrences and panda had affirmed with no fall this time.

6. The Agony

The harrowing days I have wept in,
Anguishing nights, I haven't slept in.
Some I have lost, others have vanished,
Akin a bedamn and actually being crushed.
You too will leave as did the rest,
Such thoughts drown me all along and in amidst.
Questioning Ma soul for being dutiful,
Else I wonder, am I known to that merciful?
Recalling the past, makes me weak,
Remembering the pain, while being on peak.
Ghosts of the fears buried years ago,
Concerning me afresh, so breathing low.
Indeed, had thought, of a new start,
By the discourse to be most wanted in your cart.
If even you have decided to grow apart,
Beg you for preparing me too worth in this art.

Anguished thoughts

Oh Gosh...!

All this will end like this.

Who else had thought that.

Panda-

Look, I had told you na...!

Nobody is gonna accept this all what is within us.

But...

Why?

Again that secret.

This time it was not easy to come over for Boo.

Though he tried with all he could had, but no no and only no he got from the other side...

What actually happned!

Panda gradually started ignoring the partner.

Even though they used to talk but in between there was only that tierdness and debilitation now. With the discourse of growing appart as sooner as they can for she doesn't want herself to get degraded infront of anyone for such a deed. She exclaimed!

The Boo on the other side noticing, what was aching him enough. He always tried harder with unusual wet eyes to sobb the panda but she now every time refused for a stay like as being staranger again but this time with brief memoris.

The feeling of being cursed throughout, just got that boost, what was enough to kill every admiring and favorable intuition within the boo.

For no replies, he used to type a dictionary and acting like a gluey and tacky, for he was of the view i will get that brad back.

But, seldom it matters for her now.

The promises are ment to be broken was a read, boo had never mastered.

He is still firm and standing loyal for all the assurances and vow's he had obligated.

But, can you guess?

How everything in him has changed now!

Come along.......

I'll show you,

7. The misery

Feeling the agony and the everlasting pain,
with fragmented heart, tears alike pouring rain.
How could she choose someone over me,
recolleting the pledges, she had with me.
Of course i'm fine, though just a mask,
will be relieved a little, if you just ask.
Sensing you now like out of reach,
standing alone, being mad on a sandy beach.
Awaken nights, dreadfull thoughts and a wish to change,
convincing this shaken me, for all what look strange.
Never i can, nor i dare, mending the jolted heart,
fustrated with this as entire world has fallen apart.
Though tried my hard and endeavored the best,
gave you the all and nothing left abaft and at the rest.
Had imagined ma ultimate on the onset and throughout,
desolated all, you executed ma perception barring no doubt.
Was a lad, glad and cheerful chap,
now a fail, anguished and a dreadful scrap.

Harrowing state

You rememebr!

The Boo had been Hodophile.

You Know! why so?

All coz of the past agonies and the miseries he had dealt. He throughout loved to be busy with travel and exploring the asethetics of the nature, in order to get over the gloomy outlooks, cynicism and the hopelessness.

A lad who was never vulnerable to various abuses, is now a all time hophead and an addict.

No'wr are those attractive looks, funkey style and the protective soul.

Once an evaluating bloom, now a desolating knell.

The sudden introduction and further inclination towards Panda was an action worth not to be betided.

But, in this age it is never a deed to be deprived with.

look now,

Boo-

With all wet eyes and praying hands up-

O!

The sustainer, every day thousands are lost in various tragics.

let me be the one, i can't handle this as of this time.....!

Suspense Continues.....

Aah...!

Ached i felt after i got myself up after a long sleep.

So OMG!

It was juss a dream i was in.

feeling so unusual with the suspense.....

1. What was the secret, why panda pulled out?

2. If Boo had already met with agonies in the past why this time it is affecting him more.

3. What next?

Looking for such a relieved nap again to get this suspense out.

Will catch you back with this.

Sooner!

Cheerio till then.

Quotes

"Every successful person has a painful story,
Every painful story has a successful ending,
So, accept the the pain and get ready for the success".

"Remember always,
when they can't find anything wrong with you,
they will just create it".

"We rise by lifting others up"

Message

Being in a period of high energy and great enthusiasm, youth by various faiths has been given a high status as the development of civilisations and the future of nations is in their hands.

"Indeed, they were the youths who believed in their lord, and we increased them in guidance" Al Quran

In no way shall we get worn-out for some liitle comfort, but intern we should equip ourselves with knowledge, valour and wisdom that will help and assist for everlasting relief.

Parrents right from the early age should behave more like an assistant to carve the best, instead of acting like a dictator. Throughout the teen age it's really hard for normal lad to stay focused, atleast not in current traps around that stay ready to birdlime every single auspact.